Groundwood Books / House of Anansi Press
groundwoodbooks.com

We gratefully acknowledge the Government of Canada for its financial support of our publishing program.

With the participation of the Government of Canada
Avec la participation du gouvernement du Canada | Canadä

Library and Archives Canada Cataloguing in Publication
Title: Holiday! / [written and illustrated by] Natalie Nelson.
Names: Nelson, Natalie, author, illustrator.
Identifiers: Canadiana (print) 20190153350 | Canadiana (ebook) 20190153482 | ISBN 9781773062006 (hardcover) | ISBN 9781773062013 (EPUB) | ISBN 9781773063805 (Kindle)
Classification: LCC PZ7.1.N45 Hol 2020 | DDC j813/.6—dc23

The illustrations were made with cut paper and digital collage.
Design by Michael Solomon
Printed and bound in China

MIX
Paper from responsible sources
FSC
www.fsc.org
FSC® C012700

For Sheila Barry

Monday Tuesday Wednesday Thursday

Friday Saturday Sunday

HOLI MONDAY!

BY
NATALIE NELSON

Groundwood Books
House of Anansi Press
Toronto   Berkeley

Early one morning, a strange visitor arrived.

But Holiday was already unpacking his bags.

Wednesday and Thursday heard the commotion and came over to see what all the fuss was about.

My GOODNESS, you're an interesting-looking day. I really love your hat. Where did you get it?

Next we have Friday. You'll definitely want to get to know him so he invites you to his party at the end of the week.

But secretly, Friday wondered how long this guy would be hanging around.

Saturday and Sunday yawned, then went over
to say hello.

With each introduction, Monday's face got redder and redder.

But no one did.

Monday pulled Tuesday aside.

As if on cue, Holiday made an announcement.

The unlikely trio, Monday, Wednesday and Friday, gathered in the corner.

Now that's an interesting idea.
I will definitely consider it, but only if
it's okay with everyone.

The other days looked at Monday.
She loved her spot at the beginning of the week, but even she
had to admit it might be nice to take a break now and then.

So the days of the week said goodbye to Holiday. Some days were happy to see him go. Others were already planning for his return.

And EVERYONE was ready for a nap.